The Book of Christmas

First published in Great Britain in 2004 by
Chrysalis Children's Books
an imprint of Chrysalis Books Group plc
The Chrysalis Building, Bramley Road
London W10 6SP
www.chrysalisbooks.co.uk

Compilation © Fiona Waters 2004
Illustrations © Matilda Harrison 2004
Design and layout © Chrysalis Children's Books 2004
For copyright details of the individual works please see pages 95-96

The moral right of the compiler, authors and illustrator
has been asserted

Designed by Sarah Goodwin

A CIP catalogue record for this book is available
from the British Library.

ISBN 1 84365 006 1

Set in Walbaum MT, Cochin and Adine Kirnberg Script
Printed in China

2 4 6 8 10 9 7 5 3 1

This book can be ordered direct from the publisher. Please contact
the Marketing Department. But try your bookshop first.

The Book of Christmas

Compiled by Fiona Waters

Illustrated by Matilda Harrison

Chrysalis Children's Books

Contents

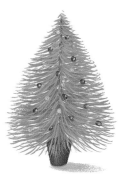

For Malcolm and Hans, with much love - F.W.

For Paul Harrison 1937-2003 - M.H.

At Nine of the Night I Opened my Door

CHARLES CAUSLEY

At nine of the night I opened my door
That stands midway between moor and moor,
And all around me, silver-bright,
I saw that the world had turned to white.

Thick was the snow on field and hedge
And vanished was the river-sedge,
Where winter skilfully had wound
A shining scarf without a sound.

And as I stood and gazed my fill
A stable-boy came down the hill.
With every step I saw him take
Flew at his heel a puff of flake.

His brow was whiter than the hoar,
A beard of freshest snow he wore,
And round about him, snowflake starred,
A red horse-blanket from the yard.

In a red cloak I saw him go,
His back was bent, his step was slow,
And as he laboured through the cold
He seemed a hundred winters old.

I stood and watched the snowy head,
The whiskers white, the cloak of red.
"A merry Christmas!" I heard him cry.
"The same to you, old friend," said I.

The Little Christ Child and the Spiders

JAN PETERS

Once upon a time, in a house near a forest lived a mother and a father, a grandmother and a grandfather, an auntie and an uncle, two children called Edward and Jane, and a dog called Benjy and a cat called Sooty. The children were very excited. For days now everyone had been getting ready for Christmas, and the house had been given such a cleaning and a polishing as never was. And there had been such a cooking and a baking as well, and the most gorgeous spicy, Christmassy smells had found their way into every corner of the house.

Edward and Jane had a lively sticky time making HEAPS of coloured paper chains, which they looped around the walls and across the rooms. Sprigs of holly were tucked behind the picture frames and a big bunch of mistletoe hung in the hall.

Now it was Christmas Eve, and tomorrow would be the Little Christ Child's birthday. That afternoon, the children went with their father, grandfather and uncle to find the most beautiful Christmas tree in the forest. They carried it home through the snow on a big toboggan. Now it stood, tall and green in a big tub in the sitting room window, waiting for the grown-ups to decorate it after the children had gone to bed.

Long after they were in bed, Edward and Jane could hear all sorts of interesting noises downstairs. They could just see their Christmas stockings hanging at the foot of their beds. It was all so exciting that they thought they would never go to sleep, but of course, at last they did.

The grown-ups had such fun decorating the Christmas tree! Finally, Father climbed the step-ladder and fixed the big star to the topmost branch. And so at last, the tree was finished, ready for Christmas morning. Uncle carried the

step-ladder out to the woodshed whilst the others tidied away the boxes and the tissue paper and string. Granny put the guard around the fire, and turned out the lights. Soon, everyone in the house was fast asleep, and it was all quiet, and dark and still...

Presently, into the house came the Little Christ Child, to see that all was well. He went into the downstairs rooms and saw how bright and clean they were. He saw the Christmas tree with its toys and candles. He went into the kitchen to see Benjy and Sooty. And then he went upstairs.

The Little Christ Child was just going into the first bedroom when he heard a strange sort of twittering noise. It seemed to be coming from the very top of the house, so he climbed up the dark, twisty stairs and went into the attic.

And what do you think he saw? SPIDERS! Lots and lots of them. And they were all talking and crying and arguing as hard as they could.

"What is the matter?" asked the Little Christ Child.

So, sniffling and snuffling, the spiders told him how every year when the house was made specially clean and shiny for his birthday, they were all turned out of their nice, warm, cosy homes downstairs. And in the sitting room there was a great big SOMETHING called a Christmas tree. They had one every year and the spiders were longing to see it. The grown-ups had seen it, Benjy and Sooty had seen it, the children would see it tomorrow and they were the only ones who had never, EVER seen it – and it wasn't fair!

"Well," said the Little Christ Child, "if you are very good and very quick, I will let you go and look at the Christmas tree, but you must promise me not to touch!"

The little spiders promised faithfully and scuttered away downstairs as fast as their legs would carry them. The Little Christ Child smiled to himself and thought "Poor little spiders!" Then he went into the bedrooms to see that all was well with the family.

When he came out, he couldn't see any spiders anywhere and he thought how very good and quick they had been. But before he left the house, the Little Christ Child thought he had better make sure those little spiders hadn't touched anything, so he went into the sitting room. And what do you think he saw?

That beautiful Christmas tree which the grown-ups had decorated so lovingly was covered from top to bottom with ... spiders' webs! The spiders had been so excited to see the Christmas tree that they had quite forgotten their promise and now there they were, climbing all over it, swinging down from branch to branch, and simply covering it with their grey, dusty cobwebs.

"Oh, you naughty little spiders!" cried the Little Christ Child. "Come down at once! Oh dear, what am I going to do?"

The little spiders scuttered down the tree as fast as they could and stood in an unhappy huddle near the door.

The Little Christ Child stood and looked at the Christmas tree and thought … and then he had an idea. He went up to the tree and gently, very gently, ran the tips of his fingers along those grey spidery webs. And when he had finished, he stood back and looked at it.

"Yes," he said, "I think that will do."

The Little Christ Child smiled at the spiders.

"Thank you, little spiders," he said. "Happy Christmas!" And he went out into the night.

The spiders gazed at the tree in amazement. Had they really helped the Little Christ Child to do this special magic? Then, whispering to each other about what they had seen, they scuttled back to their own warm, cosy homes once more.

Christmas morning came at last!

Edward and Jane rushed in and out of all the bedrooms singing, laughing and shouting, "Happy Christmas!" and "Can we see the tree now?" Everyone gathered outside the sitting room, Father flung open the door and they all crowded inside.

What a sight met their eyes! All those grey spidery webs had turned into long, shining, shimmering silver strands. For a while they were too astounded to move. Then, a little cautiously at first, they went up to the tree and gently touched the sparkling threads.

"Oh, how beautiful!" they said. "But what are they and how did they get there?"

Nobody knew. But we know, don't we?

And so, of course, did the spiders!

How Far

NAT GOULD

The old man trudges patiently,
The donkey after him
With neat hoof.
The old man throats a temple chant
Flatvoice
Under his breath.
Gnarled hand holds
A drooping cord.
It swings.
Worn
Soft as a loving word
It hangs strong as a bronze door ton-down
      Onto a hinge,
Light as a cobweb holding chasm sides together,
Homely as a rough robe tassel,
Safe as a sandal-thong.

The animal treads dainty,
Hooves tocking on pebbles,
Scrambling in sand,
Prints scumbled by dust.
Long ears point
The flat-note temple tune,
The pitch-intent, the words.

Follow,
The way is long, – How long?
How far to Egypt
From these arid scapes
More friend than foe-Jerusalem,
Less woe than Bethlehem.

Country Carol

SUE COWLING

Walked on the crusted grass in the frosty air.
Blackbird saw me, gave me a gold-rimmed stare.

Walked in the winter woods where the snow lay deep.
Hedgehog heard me, smiled at me in his sleep.

Walked by the frozen pond where the ice shone pale.
Wind sang softly, moon dipped its silver sail.

Walked on the midnight hills till the star-filled dawn.
No one told me, I knew a king was born.

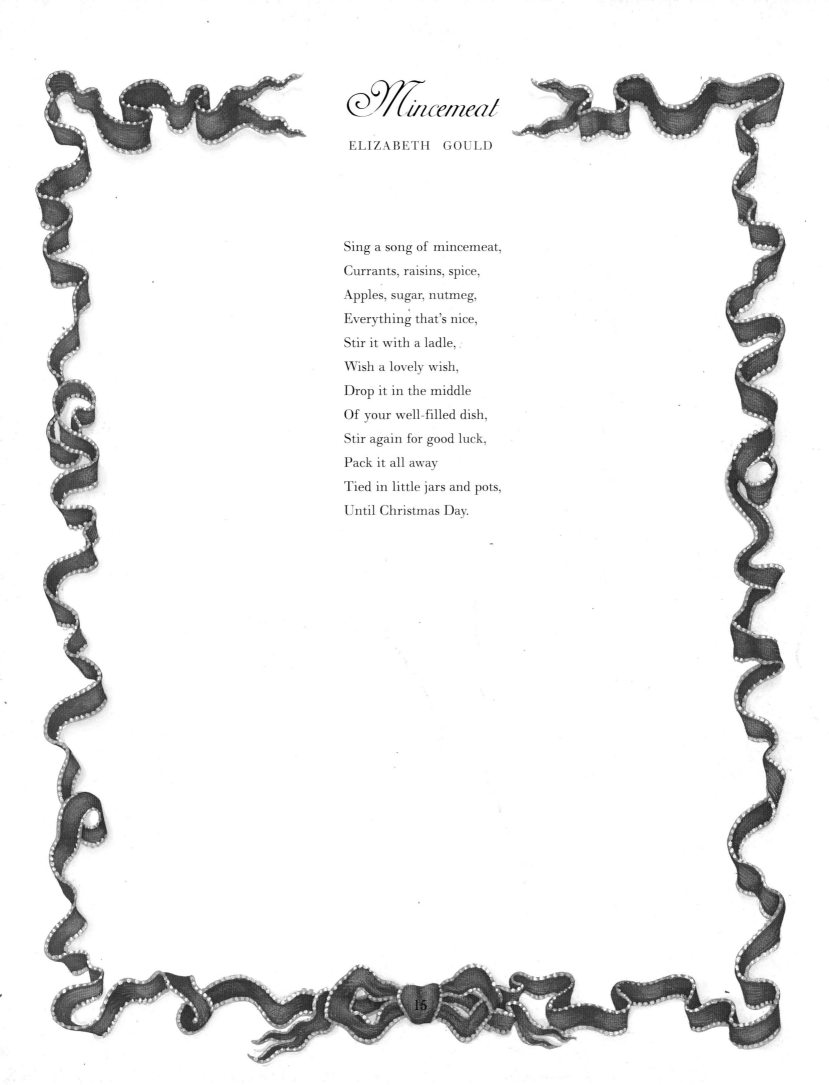

Mincemeat

ELIZABETH GOULD

Sing a song of mincemeat,
Currants, raisins, spice,
Apples, sugar, nutmeg,
Everything that's nice,
Stir it with a ladle,
Wish a lovely wish,
Drop it in the middle
Of your well-filled dish,
Stir again for good luck,
Pack it all away
Tied in little jars and pots,
Until Christmas Day.

Nativity Play

PETER DIXON

This year ...
This year can I be Herod?
This year, can I be him?
A wise man
or a Joseph?
An inn man
or a king?

This year ...
can I be famous?
This year, can I be best?
Bear a crown of silver
and wear a golden vest?

This year ...
can I be starlight?
This year, can I stand out?

... feel the swish of curtains
and hear the front row shout
"Hurrah" for good old Ronny
he brings a gift of gold
head afire with tinsel
"The Greatest Story Told ..."
"Hurrah for good old Herod!"
and shepherds from afar.

So –
don't make me a palm tree
And can I be –

a Star?

Cat in the Manger

U A FANTHORPE

In the story, I'm not there.
Ox and ass, arranged at prayer:
But me? Nowhere.

Anti-cat evangelists
How on earth could you have missed
Such an obvious and able
Occupant of any stable?

Who excluded mouse and rat?
The harmless necessary cat.
Who snuggled in with the holy pair?
Me. And my purr.

Matthew, Mark and Luke and John
(Who got it wrong,
Who left out the cat)
Remember that,
Wherever He went in this great affair,
I was there.

The King and Queen of Christmas

JOHN RICE

High above house,
high above hill.
Through the clouds and further still.

Beyond the moon
and past the sun
to where the silent comets run:

it is here that the Queen of Christmas
and the Christmas King
travel among the constellations in bubbles of air.

They carry books, strange musical instruments
and white umbrellas that are
sprinkled with the dust of dark stars.
They have strands of amber in their hair.
Their eyes are a distant blue, like far-off mountains.
Their silky robes flow like soft stream water.
Jewels fall from their deep sleeves —
apples and pears too.

When springtime approaches
they wear emerald-green crowns
and playing their strange music
they call the world alive.

18

In the early days of summer
they put on crimson clothes
and sing the bright dawn anew.
They have sharp voices, like birds.

In swirling autumn winds
they rescue the reddy-brown leaves
and wear them tangled in the webs of their white hair.

But the winter wild is their true season:
because when Orion the Hunter marches
across the sky, the King and Queen of Christmas
cast off their bright colours
and dress themselves in black capes
fringed with silver clasps, adorned with gold brooches.
And with a finger ring of sharp diamonds
they pierce their bubble homes
and soar and soar and soar
through the clouds of space dust
like dark doves in the solar wind.
Occasionally they have to stop to wipe their eyes.
Then, in the middle of their winter world,
on Christmas Eve, on the first chime of midnight,
the Queen of Christmas and the Christmas King
take the new moon, sharp as a blade,
and slit the wrapping paper sky.

They help each other parcel up frosty stars.
The King takes a string of star-pearls
to tie the parcel. The Queen stretches out
her sparkling hand and grasps
a passing comet to use as a gift-tag.
The Queen of Christmas and the Christmas King
then carry this special present on a long journey:

19

they slide past the icy meteorites,

they glide between glassy suns,

they slink in and out of the doors of the deep cosmos,

they skim the edges of planets' rings,

making their way through

the colourful caves and caverns of endless space,

to this shining Earth

to this cold country

to this snowy town

to this still and peaceful street,

to this sleeping house,

to this quiet bedroom,

to this soft bed

and place their skygift on your pillow,

as gently as moonlight falls on a pond.

And PING!

the second you open your eyes on Christmas morn

the dark blue parcel bursts open without a sound

and showers you with the frosty stars

that zing and spin and split and melt and vanish

to become tiny bubbles of Happy Christmasness.

And no one sees the Queen of Christmas

and the Christmas King smile

as they travel in their bubbles of air

back to where night and her train of stars

colour another world.

Lullay My Liking

FIFTEENTH-CENTURY CAROL

Lullay, my liking, my son, my sweeting.
Lullay, my dear heart, my own dear darling.

I saw a fair maiden
Sit and sing:
She lulled a little child,
A sweet lording.

He is that Lord
Who made every thing:
Of all lords the Lord,
Of all kings the King.

There was much song
At that child's birth:
All those in heaven,
They made much mirth.

Angels bright, they sung that night,
And said to that child:
"Blessed be thou and so be she,
That is both meek and mild."

Pray we now to that child
And to his mother dear,
To bless us all
Who now made cheer.

Lullay, my liking, my son, my sweeting.
Lullay, my dear heart, my own dear darling.

The Mayor and the Simpleton

IAN SERRAILLIER

They followed the Star to Bethlehem –
Boolo the baker, Barleycorn the farmer,
old Darby and Joan, a small boy Peter, and
a simpleton whose name was Innocent.
Over the snowfields and the frozen rutted lanes
they followed the Star to Bethlehem.

Innocent stood at the stable door
and watched them enter. A flower
stuck out of his yellow hair; his mouth gaped open
like a drawer that wouldn't shut.
He beamed upon the child where he lay
among the oxen, in swaddling clothes in the hay,
his blue eyes shining steady as the Star overhead;
beside him old Joseph and
Mary his mother, smiling.

> Innocent was delighted.

They brought gifts with them – Boolo, some fresh crusty loaves
(warm from the baking) which he laid
at the feet of the infant Jesus, kneeling
in all humility.

> Innocent was delighted.

Barleycorn brought two baskets – one with a dozen eggs,
the other with two chickens – which he laid
at the feet of the infant Jesus, kneeling
in all humility.

> Innocent was delighted.

Darby and Joan brought apples and pears from their garden,

wrapped in her apron and stuffed

in the pockets of his trousers; the little boy

a pot of geraniums – he had grown them himself.

And they laid them

at the feet of the infant Jesus, kneeling

in all humility.

Innocent was delighted.

The mayor rolled up in his coach with a jingle of bells

and a great to-do. He stepped out with a flourish

and fell flat on his face in the snow. His footmen

picked him up and opened his splendid

crimson umbrella. Then he strutted to the door,

while the white flakes floated down

and covered it with spots. He was proud of his umbrella

and didn't mean to give it away.

Shaking the snow off on to the stable floor,

the mayor peered down at the child where he lay

among the oxen, in swaddling clothes in the hay,

his blue eyes shining steady as the Star overhead,

beside him old Joseph and

Mary his mother, smiling.

Innocent was puzzled.

And the mayor said: "On this important occasion

each must take a share in the general thanksgiving.

Hence the humble gifts – the very humble gifts –

which I see before me. My own contribution

is something special – a speech. I made it up myself and I'm sure

you'll all like it. Ahem. Pray silence for the mayor."

"Moo, moo," said the oxen.

"My fellow citizens,

the happy event I refer to — in which we all rejoice —

has caused a considerable stir

in the parish — "

" — in the whole world," said a voice.

Who spoke? Could it be Innocent, always so shy,

timid as a butterfly, frightened

as a sparrow with a broken wing? Yes, it was he.

Now God had made him bold.

"I fear I must start again," said the mayor.

"My fellow citizens, in the name of the people of this parish

I am proud to welcome one

who promises so well — "

" — He is the Son of Heaven,"

said Innocent.

The mayor took no notice.

"I prophesy a fine future for him,

almost — you might say — spectacular.

He'll do us all credit. At the same time I salute in particular

the child's mother, the poor woman who — "

" — She is not poor but the richest, most radiant

of mothers."

"Simpleton, how dare you interrupt!"

snapped the mayor.

But God, who loves the humble, heard him not.

He made him listen, giving Innocent the words:

"Mr Mayor, you don't understand. This birth

is no local event. The child is Jesus,

King of kings and Lord of lords.

A stable is his place and poverty his dwelling-place —

yet he has come to save the world. No speech

is worthy of him — "

"Tush!" said the mayor.
"I took a lot of trouble. It's a rare
and precious gift, my speech — and now
I can't get a word in edgeways."
"Rare and precious, did you say? Hear what the child
has brought to us — peace on earth, goodwill toward men.
O truly rare and precious gift!"
"Peace on earth," said the neighbours,
"goodwill toward men. O truly rare
and precious gift!" They knelt in humility,
in gratitude to the child who lay
among the oxen, in swaddling clothes in the hay,
his blue eyes shining steady as the Star overhead,
beside him old Joseph and
Mary his mother, smiling.

The mayor was silent. God gave the simpleton
no more to say. Now
like a frightened bird
over the snowfields and the frozen rutted lanes
he fluttered away. Always, as before, a flower
stuck out of his yellow hair; his mouth gaped open
like a drawer that wouldn't shut.
He never spoke out like that again.

As for the mayor, he didn't finish his speech.
He called for his coach and drove off, frowning,
much troubled. For a little while
he thought of what the simpleton had said
But he soon forgot all about it, having
important business to attend to in town.

Three Kings Came Riding

HENRY WADSWORTH LONGFELLOW

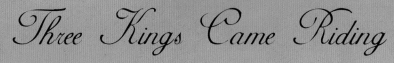

Three Kings came riding from far away,
Melchior and Gaspar and Baltasar;
Three Wise Men out of the East were they,
And they travelled by night and they slept by day,
For their guide was a beautiful, wonderful star.

The star was so beautiful, large and clear,
That all the other stars of the sky
Became a white mist in the atmosphere,
And by this they knew that the coming was near
Of the Prince foretold in the prophecy.

Three caskets they bore on their saddle-bows,
Three caskets of gold with golden keys;
Their robes were of crimson silk, with rows
Of bells and pomegranates and furbelows,
Their turbans like blossoming almond-trees.

And so the Three Kings rode into the West,
Through the dusk of night, over hill and dell,
And sometimes they nodded, with beard on breast,
And sometimes talked, as they paused to rest,
With the people they met at some wayside well.

"Of the child that is born," said Baltasar,
"Good people, I pray you, tell us the news;
For we in the East have seen his star,
And have ridden fast, and have ridden far,
To find and worship the King of the Jews."

And the people answered, "You ask in vain;
We know of no king but Herod the Great!
They thought the Wise Men were men insane,
As they spurred their horses across the plain,
Like riders in haste, and who cannot wait.

And when they came to Jerusalem,
Herod the Great, who had heard this thing,
Sent for the Wise Men and questioned them;
And said, "Go down unto Bethlehem,
And bring me tidings of this new king."

So they rode away; and the star stood still,
The only one in the grey of the morn;
Yes, it stopped, it stood still of its own free will,
Right over Bethlehem on the hill,
The city of David where Christ was born.

And the Three Kings rode through the gate and the guard,
Through the silent street, till their horses turned
And neighed as they entered the great inn-yard;
But the windows were closed, and the doors were barred,
And only a light in the stable burned.

And cradled there in the scented hay,
In the air made sweet by the breath of kine,
The little child in the manger lay,
The child that would be King one day
Of a kingdom not human but divine.

His mother, Mary of Nazareth,
Sat watching beside his place of rest,
Watching the even flow of his breath,
For the joy of life and the terror of death
Were mingled together in her breast.

They laid their offerings at his feet;
The gold was their tribute to a King,
The frankincense, with its odour sweet,
Was for the Priest, the Paraclete,
The myrrh for the body's burying.

And the mother wondered and bowed her head,
And sat as still as a statue of stone;
Her heart was troubled yet comforted,
Remembering what the Angel had said,
Of an endless reign and of David's throne.

Then the Kings rode out of the city gate,
With a clatter of hoofs in proud array;
But they went not back to Herod the Great,
For they knew his malice and feared his hate,
And returned to their homes by another way.

The Christmas Life

WENDY COPE

If you don't have a real tree, you don't
bring the Christmas life into the house.
Josephine Mackinnon, aged 8

Bring in a tree, a young Norwegian spruce,
Bring hyacinths that rooted in the cold,
Bring winter jasmine as its buds unfold:
Bring the Christmas life into this house.

Bring red and green and gold, bring things that shine,
Bring candlesticks and music, food and wine.
Bring in your memories of Christmas past,
Bring in your tears for all that you have lost.

Bring in the shepherd boy, the ox and ass,
Bring in the stillness of an icy night,
Bring in a birth, of hope and love and light:
Bring the Christmas life into this house.

Stable Song

JUDITH NICHOLLS

She lies, a stillness in the crumpled straw
Whilst he looks softly on the child, unsure,
And shadows waver by the stable door.

The oxen stir; a moth drifts through the bare
Outbuilding, silken Gabriel-winged, to where
She lies, a stillness in the crumpled straw.

A carpenter, his wife, both unaware
That kings and shepherds seek them from afar
And shadows waver by the stable door.

The child sleeps on. A drowse of asses snore;
He murmurs gently, raises eyes to her
Who lies, a stillness in the crumpled straw.

A cockerel crows, disturbed by sudden fear
As shepherds, dark upon the hill, appear
And shadows waver by the stable door.

The hush of birth is in the midnight air
And new life hides the distant smell of myrrh;
She lies, a stillness in the crumpled straw,
And shadows waver by the stable door.

Christmas at Green Knowe

LUCY M BOSTON

That night there was neither thunder nor snow, but a bright moon and keen frost. Before starting to walk to Midnight Mass with Mrs Oldknow, Tolly had been privately to look at St Christopher. The moon shone full on his weathered stone face. He looked as if he had not moved since the beginning of time. As they set off with their moon shadows playing on the path round their feet, Tolly wondered if Linnet was looking out of the top window.

His shadow had long legs that he was rather proud of.

"Granny," he said, "your shadow looks just like a partridge."

"I've often thought you don't always know whose shadow comes out with you."

They were going to the church where Toby and Alexander had sung in the choir, where St Christopher had knelt unseen among the cypresses and tombstones.

The footpath went along beside the river, through wide flat meadows.

It was surrounded by miles and miles of silent moonlight. There was almost no view but sky. Tolly had not yet been to the church; he imagined it as the most beautiful and exciting end to a thrilling walk. In fact he was confusing it in his mind with that other church where Alexander had experimented with echoes and which he had called JOYOUS GARD. In the moonlight the frozen meadows looked like sheets of frosted glass and the river like gold, old gold full of black creases like Linnet's bracelet when they were cleaning it. The cold made an eerie humming in the telegraph wires, a sound that grew suddenly alarmingly loud if Tolly put his ear against the post. There were no lights showing from any cottage window, not any living creature out in the countryside but themselves. It was a long walk: it took them an hour and felt like a pilgrimage, but they saw nobody else going the same way. Tolly began to feel that he and his great-grandmother were going secretly to meet Toby and Alexander and perhaps their father and mother; that it was to be a mysterious and delightful family affair.

When they came inside the church, the first impression that he received was the mixed smell of incense and clammy mould, with the mould predominating. There were a few other people there, dingy, unromantic townsfolk, no children at all. The church was battered and dank, festooned with cobwebs round the windows, carpeted like a kitchen with brown coconut matting and bleakly lit with electric light. It is true that on the altar there were candles and chrysanthemums, but he could not help feeling that it was ugly and disappointing. There was a huge picture hanging on the wall on his left that was so horrifying that he kept one hand up to the side of his face like a blinker in case he should see it by accident. When they stood up to sing, the organ wheezed out as if it were the funeral march for a cat. Tolly was afraid to hear his own voice above the faint caterwauling that dragged after it. He was tired and felt suddenly very sad. Finally he fell asleep against Mrs Oldknow's shoulder.

When he opened his eyes, the electric light was out and far more candles were burning. The church looked new. The stone, instead of being grey, stained with black damp, was a nice sandy colour. The pews had gone. The pillars rose out of the floor like tree-trunks, leaving the nave spacious and gay. Instead of the wheezy organ there was a sound of fiddles and trumpets. People came in walking freely as if to a party, and stood in groups here and there.

Tolly turned round at a clinking sound close behind him, and there was Toby walking in with his mother on his arm. He was wearing his sword. When he had placed his mother near Mrs Oldknow he bowed formally to them and went out again. His place was taken by someone who could only be a Boggis, who stood respectfully just behind young Mrs Oldknow. She smiled at the old lady and at Tolly, raising one eyebrow at him as if to say, "You here too?"

When at last he could take his eyes off her and look towards the choir, the boys were just coming in. There were six of them in surplices with white frills round their necks. Two little boys came first.

One was laughing and turned to look at them as he went by. Alexander and a stranger came next, and then Toby and another, and after them the men. But Tolly was looking at the first little boy who just could not be solemn, for he knew now that it was Linnet, dressed in boy's clothes, in church, in the choir. He looked anxiously at Mrs Oldknow, fearing to see a look of angry shame come over her face, but she was looking at her book and smiling. He nudged his great-grandmother but she only laid her fingers on her lips and put her hand through his arm.

The singing was beautiful. Tolly knew it was part-singing, but he could only hear all four notes when there was a pause and they all hung together on the air. It gave him pleasure almost painful. Sometimes Toby sang solo for a few minutes and sometimes Alexander. His voice flew up to the roof as easily as a bird. Tolly feared it would make him cry, but that passed off when he saw Linnet hitching up her trousers. They were probably Alexander's and too big for her.

Then, gazing round the church, he saw, or thought he saw, through the wavering candle shadows, leaning against the wall, as much a part of it and as little noticed as if he were at home, St Christopher himself. Linnet was almost opposite him. She made signs that Tolly did not understand until he craned up to see better. Then he saw, pressed against the stone ripples that washed St Christopher's feet, the little black-and-white dog Orlando, fixing obedient eyes on his mistress and thumping the floor with his tail. Tolly gave a little squeak of laughter, but it was luckily drowned in the peal of bells that broke out.

Mrs Oldknow said: "Wake up, Tolly. A Happy Christmas to you! We are going back in my friend's car, so you will soon be in bed. Did you have nice dreams?"

Tolly looked quite bewildered. "Yes, Granny," he said. "Were you asleep too?"

"Perhaps," she said. "I hardly know."

The Waiting Game

JOHN MOLE

Nuts and marbles in the toe,
An orange in the heel,
A Christmas stocking in the dark
Is wonderful to feel.

Shadowy, bulging length of leg
That crackles when you clutch,
A Christmas stocking in the dark
Is marvellous to touch.

You lie back on your pillow
But that shape's still hanging there.
A Christmas stocking in the dark
Is very hard to bear,

So try to get to sleep again
And chase the hours away.
A Christmas stocking in the dark
Must wait for Christmas Day.

Pudding Charms

CHARLOTTE DRUITT COLE

Our Christmas pudding was made in November,
All they put in it, I quite well remember:
Currants and raisins, and sugar and spice,
Orange peel, lemon peel – everything nice
Mixed up together, and put in a pan.
"When you've stirred it," said Mother, "as much as you can,
We'll cover it over, that nothing may spoil it,
And then, in the copper, tomorrow we'll boil it."
That night, when we children were all fast asleep,
A real fairy godmother came crip-a-creep!

She wore a red cloak, and a tall steeple hat
(Though nobody saw her but Tinker, the cat!)
And out of her pocket a thimble she drew,
A button of silver, a silver horse-shoe,
And, whisp'ring a charm in the pudding pan popped them,
Then flew up the chimney directly she dropped them;
And even old Tinker pretended he slept
(With Tinker a secret is sure to be kept!),
So nobody knew, until Christmas came round,
And there, in the pudding, these treasures we found.

We Three Camels

JANE YOLEN

I carried a king,
But not the Child,
Through desert storms
And winds so wild
The sands crept into
Every pack.
But never did
My king look back.
"Forward!" he cried,
"We follow the star,
We do not stop."
So here we are.

I carried a king,
But not the One,
Through searing heat
And blinding sun,
Through nights so cold
My nostrils froze,
And slaves wrapped
cloths
About my toes.
But forward we went
Led by a star.
We did not stop,
So here we are.

I carried a king,
But not the Babe,
And also boxes
Jewel inlaid.
My packs were stuffed
With scents and spice,
The grandest ladies
To entice.
No ladies saw we,
But only a star.
We did not stop
So here we are.

Shepherd's Carol

NORMAN NICHOLSON

Three practical farmers from back of the dale –
      Under the high sky –
On a Saturday night said "So long" to their sheep
That were bottom of the dyke and fast asleep –
      When the stars came out in the Christmas sky.

They called at the pub for a gill of ale –
      Under the high sky –
And they found in the stable, stacked with the corn,
The latest arrival, newly-born –
      When the stars came out in the Christmas sky.

They forgot their drink, they rubbed their eyes –
      Under the high sky –
They were tough as leather and ripe as a cheese
But they dropped like a ten-year-old down on their knees –
      When the stars came out in the Christmas sky.

They ran out in the yard to swap their news –
      Under the high sky –
They pulled off their caps and roused a cheer
To greet a spring lamb before New Year –
      When the stars came out in the Christmas sky.

The Thorn

HELEN DUNMORE

There was no berry on the bramble
only the thorn,
there was no rose, not one petal,
only the bare thorn
the night he was born.

There was no wind to guide them,
only the wind's whistling,
there was no light in the stable,
only the starshine
and a candle guttering
the night he was born.

From nothing and nowhere
this couple came,
at every border
their papers were wrong
but they reached the city
and begged for a room.

There was no berry on the bramble,
no rose, not one petal,
only the thorn,
and a cold wind whispering
the night he was born.

Making the Most of It

WILLIAM KEAN SEYMOUR

For twelve days and nights
The Christmas Tree that I bought last year
Stood unwatered and undernourished
In a flower-pot in the drawing-room.
How could we know what it felt,
Hung with coloured globes and tinsel,
Gifts and candles;
Pulled and poked about and fingered
By eager children;
Wreathed with smoke from cigars and cigarettes
And fumes of wine and punch?

When the Feast was over
I took a chance
And carefully replanted the tree in my garden,
Tenderly spreading the parched and aching roots,
Not daring to think he might live:
But he did.

Now he comes back into the house again,
Like an old servant called in for a special occasion,
Glad to be made use of,
Beaming upon the company from the serving table.

Of course I am not sure I have done the right thing.
He may catch cold, or catch warm (which is worse),
For it can't be good for trees to be dug up annually
And draped with 'frost', and tinsel,
Gleaming balls and candles,
And made to stand in sand for twelve days and nights.

We shouldn't like it if we were Christmas trees!
The only thing to do is to give him a third chance
And hope he will take it.

The Cherry Tree Carol

ANONYMOUS APPALACHIAN FOLK SONG

As Joseph and Mary were a-walking the green,
They was apples and cherries plenty there to be seen.
And then Mary said to Joseph, so meek and so mild:

Gather me some cherries, Joseph, for I am with child.

Then Joseph said to Mary so rough and unkind:

Let the daddy of the baby get the cherries for thine.

Then the baby spoke out of its mother's womb:

Bow down you lofty cherry trees, let my mammy have some.

Then the cherry tree bent and it bowed like a bow,
So that Mary picked cherries from the uppermost bough.
Then Joseph took Mary all on his left knee,
Saying:

Lord have mercy on me and what I have done.

Then Joseph took Mary on
his right knee, Saying:

O my little Saviour, when your birthday shall be,
The hills and the mountains shall bow unto thee.

Then the baby spoke out
of its mother's womb:

On old Christmas morning my birthday shall be,
When the hills and high mountains shall bow unto me.

Christmas Ornaments

VALERIE WORTH

The boxes break
At the corners,
Their sides
Sink weak;

They are tied up
Every year
With the same
Grey string;

But under the split
Lids, a fortune
Shines: globes
Of gold and sapphire,

Silver spires and
Bells, jewelled
Nightingales with
Pearly tails.

Snapdragon

ANONYMOUS

Here he comes with flaming bowl,
Don't he mean to take his toll,
Snip! Snap! Dragon.
Take care you don't take too much,
Be not greedy in your clutch,
Snip! Snap! Dragon.

With his blue and lapping tongue
Many of you will be stung,
Snip! Snap! Dragon.
For he snaps at all that comes
Snatching at his feast of plums,
Snip! Snap! Dragon.

But old Christmas makes him come,
Though he looks so fee! fo! fum!
Snip! Snap! Dragon.
Don't 'ee fear him, but be bold,
Out he goes, his flames are cold,
Snip! Snap! Dragon.

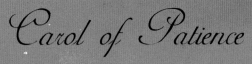

Carol of Patience

ROBERT GRAVES

Shepherds armed with staff and sling,
Ranged along a steep hillside
Watch for their anointed King
By all prophets prophesied —
    Sing patience, patience,
    Only still have patience.

Hour by hour they scrutinize
Comet, planet, planet, star,
Till the oldest shepherd sighs,
"I am frail and he is far."
    Sing patience, patience,
    Only still have patience.

"Born, they say, a happy child;
Grown, a man of grief to be,
From all careless joys exiled,
Rooted in eternity."
    Sing patience, patience,
    Only still have patience.

Then another shepherd said:
"Yonder lights are Bethlehem;
There young David raised his head
Destined for the diadem."
    Sing patience, patience,
    Only still have patience.

Cried the youngest shepherd: "There
Our Redeemer comes tonight,
Comes with starlight on his hair,
With his brow exceeding bright."
Sing patience, patience,
Only still have patience.

"Sacrifice no lamb nor kid,
Let such foolish fashions pass;
In a manger find him hid,
Breathed upon by ox and ass."
Sing patience, patience,
Only still have patience.

Dance for him and laugh and sing,
Watch him mercifully smile,
Dance although tomorrow bring
Every plague that plagued the Nile.
Sing patience, patience,
Only still have patience.

Somewhere around Christmas

JOHN SMITH

Always, or nearly always, on old apple trees,

Somewhere around Christmas, if you look up through the frost,

You will see, fat as a bullfinch, stuck on a high branch,

One, lingering, bald, self-sufficient, hard, blunt fruit.

There will be no leaves, you can be sure of that;

The twigs will be tar-black, and the white sky

Will be grabbed among the branches like thumbed glass

In broken triangles just saved from crashing to the ground.

Further up, dribbles of rain will run down

Like spilt colourless varnish on a canvas. The old tins,

Tyres, cardboard boxes, debris of back gardens,

Will lie around, bleak, with mould and rust creeping over them.

Blow on your fingers. Wipe your feet on the mat by the back door.

You will never see that apple fall. Look at the cat,

Her whiskers twitch as she sleeps by the kitchen fire;

In her backyard prowling dream she thinks it's a bird.

The Three Drovers

JOHN   WHEELER

Across the plains one Christmas night, three drovers
  riding blythe and gay,
Looked up and saw a starry light, more radiant than
  the Milky Way;
And on their hearts such wonder fell, they sang with
  joy "Noel! Noel!"

The air was dry with summer heat, and smoke was
  on the yellow moon;
But from the heavens, faint and sweet, came floating
  down a wondrous tune;
And, as they heard, they sang full well, those drovers
  three "Noel! Noel!"

The black swans flew across the sky, the wild dog
  called across the plain,
The starry lustre blazed on high, still echoed on the
  heavenly strain;
And still they sang "Noel! Noel!" those drovers three
  "Noel! Noel!"

Ghost Story

DYLAN THOMAS

Bring out the tall tales now that we told
by the fire as the gaslight bubbled like a diver.
Ghosts whooed like owls in the long nights
when I dared not look over my shoulder; animals
lurked in the cubbyhole under the stairs where the
gas meter ticked. And I remember that we went
singing carols once, when there wasn't the shaving
of a moon to light the flying streets. At the end
of a long road was a drive that led to a large
 house, and we stumbled up the darkness of the drive
  that night, each one of us afraid, each one holding
  a stone in his hand in case, and all of us too brave
  to say a word. The wind through the trees
  made noises as of old and unpleasant and maybe
  webfooted men wheezing in caves. We reached
  the black bulk of the house,
 "What shall we give them? Hark the Herald?"
 "No," Jack said, "Good King Wenceslas.
 I'll count three."
One, two, three, and we began to sing.

Our voices high and seemingly distant in the
snow-felted darkness around the house that
was occupied by nobody we knew. We stood
close together, near the dark door.
"Good King Wenceslas looked out
On the Feast of Stephen …"
And then a small, dry voice, like the voice
of someone who has not spoken for a long time,
joined our singing: a small dry eggshell voice
from the other side of the door: a small dry voice
through the keyhole. And when we stopped running
we were outside our house; the front room was lovely:
balloons floated under the hot-water-bottle-gulping gas;
everything was good again and shone over the town.
"Perhaps it was a ghost," Jim said.
"Perhaps it was trolls," Dan said,
who was always reading.

"Let's go in and see if there's any jelly left,"
Jack said. And we did that.

Little Tree

E E CUMMINGS

little tree

little silent Christmas tree

you are so little

you are more like a flower

who found you in the green forest

and were you very sorry to come away?

see   i will comfort you

because you smell so sweetly

i will kiss your cool bark

and hug you safe and tight

just as your mother would,

only don't be afraid

look   the spangles

that sleep all the year in a dark box

dreaming of being taken out and allowed to shine,

the balls the chains red and gold the fluffy threads,

put up your little arms

and i'll give them all to you to hold

every finger shall have its ring

and there won't be a single place dark or unhappy

then when you're quite dressed

you'll stand in the window for everyone to see

and how they'll stare!

oh but you'll be very proud

and my little sister and i will take hands

and looking up at our beautiful tree

we'll dance and sing

"Noel Noel"

The Sheepdog

U A FANTHORPE

After the very bright light,
And the talking bird,
And the singing,
And the sky filled up wi' wings,
And then the silence,

Our lads sez
We'd better go, then.
Stay, Shep. Good dog, stay.
So I stayed wi' t' sheep.

After they cum back,
It sounded grand, what they'd seen:
Camels, and kings, and such,
Wi' presents – human sort,
Not the kind you eat –
And a baby. Presents wes for him.
Our lads took him a lamb.

I had to stay behind wi' t' sheep.
Pity they didn't tek me along too.
I'm good wi' lambs,
And the baby might have liked a dog
After all that myrrh and such.

Jubilate Herbis

NORMA FARBER

Let Christmas celebrate greenly. For the fir is king of the forest. Glorify with laurel. Loop it into thornless branches.

Extol holly, compliment the greeness and redness both. Husband or wife, whichever first brings it, shall rule this house. For holly is a ward of the sun, warrant of spring's return.

Commend yellow bedstraw, whereon Mary rested. It fairly bursts its buds to welcome the birth. For this, the colour of the petals deepened from pallor to gold.

Rejoice with spike-bloomed sainfoin. Recall how it bent down its stalk: dry bedding for the babe. When Mary laid him upon it, the manger lighted up, a garden.

Honour hellebore, that it sprang to flower for shepherd girl. Even the Magi brought no such riches.

Magnify rosemary, for it sheltered Mary on the road into Egypt. Acclaim it as an herb of bitterish savour. For its pungence transfigures the humblest supper.

Laud ivy, for games, felicity, fertility, honour. Let it garland your doorways and outer passages.

Approve the lowly ground pine. Gather it with compassion, for it dresses wounds.

Applaud poinsettia, its scarlet involucre, no blood brighter.

Remember to mention mistletoe, growing in air. It merits to be harvested with a golden sickle. The hang of its waxen cloud exalts this house.

The Holly Bears a Berry

ALISON UTTLEY

It was December, the fields were bare, and the sheep were safe in the folds. The great woods spread their rimed network of branches over the little ice-covered pools. Flocks of chaffinches darted through the crystal air, playing their winter game of hide-and-seek in their favourite trees. A little brook tinkled cheerfully as it ran through ice flakes and ferny snow-flowers.

A young man walked along the narrow tracks in the woodland. In his hand was a bill-hook and on his back a rope. He wore a brown coat the colour of the dead beech leaves and his fustian trousers were tied at the knees. Round his neck was a scarf as blue as his eyes. He was seeking holly, for he had promised his young wife that he would get her a bunch of berries for Christmas.

"You'll not find one berry," she said laughing at him, as she stood at the door of the cottage by the wood. "There's ne'er a red berry this year. I've kept my eyes open when I've been out walking, but I've never seen a glimmer of one. We've got ivy and yew and bay, and we must be content with holly leaves."

"I'll find a berry for you, Jenny, sure as I'm a woodman. It wouldn't be Christmas with no holly berries to decorate the kitchen. There will surely be some in the forest on the old trees I know far away. I'll give you a surprise, Jenny Wren."

She laughed again at his words. Jenny Wren was Timothy's name for her, for he said she was as spry as a little bird and she sang as sweetly as any wren in the hedge as she went about her work in the kitchen.

"Goodbye, Jenny Wren," called Timothy, and away he went into the wood.

Jenny went back to the kitchen to scrub the table white as a bone, and polish the handles of the chest, and prepare for Christmas. The room was as neat as a little bird's nest, with warm curtains and shutters, and little rugs on the floor. There was a good fire burning, and by the side of it was a cradle. Jenny stooped over it, and rocked it for a few minutes, singing very softly.

There lay her baby son, young Timothy. It was his first Christmas, and it was fitting that everything should be beautiful for him.

So Jenny baked a batch of new bread, and filled the mince pies and sang a carol to her baby, while Timothy went on his quest.

Timothy walked boldly into the woods, making for the grove of holly trees which had been spangled with ripe berries in other years. When he reached the dark green trees he was disappointed. They stood serene, glittering in the wintry sunshine with a point of light on every sharp leaf, but never a berry grew there. Timothy searched them, but he had no reward. He went on, farther into the woods, taking a bearing of his direction now and again, tracking the hollies which grew in friendly companies here and there. He walked for miles, and the feeling of disappointment deepened. He couldn't bear to return empty-handed. It was strange that there were no holly berries in the crowds of trees which lived in the vast woods.

Then he saw a gold-crested bird with green plumage and scarlet wing feathers flying through the trees. It rested on a holly, and as he crept up to it he saw that the tree was covered with fruit which the bird was devouring. He raised his hand to scare it away, and then he stopped. It was so beautiful he had not the heart to disturb it. On Christmas Eve such a bird must surely be a sacred bird, perhaps flown from the East with the Wise Men, a part of the miracle of Christmas. So he watched the bird as it hopped among the glossy leaves and stripped the tree.

The bird watched him also, its bright eyes stared unwinking at him, it turned its head and showed off its brilliant plumage. It flirted its tail feathers and ruffled its wings as if to display all its beauty.

"I'll tell Jenny Wren about it. Never was there such a bird! It must have flown from foreign lands, from India, or China, or the hills of Bethlehem," said Timothy to himself.

Then he was aware that somebody besides himself was watching the bird. Under the tree stood a man, shadowed by the green boughs. He wore a green pointed hood on his head and green leather jacket and long jackboots. Over his shoulder was a fleece of white wool or snow, Timothy could not be sure, but it glistened like hoar-frost in the sun. His face was wrinkled and old, creased and puckered in a thousand brown lines. He held a staff in his hand, and Timothy saw that it was made of holly wood. It was spiked with broken branches, and the bark was stripped to show the white wood in a pattern of green and white. His hands were thin and his fingers were sharp as a bird's claws.

He began to sing in a clear voice, sweet as an angel's

The holly and the ivy,

When they are both full grown,

Of all the trees that are in the wood

The holly bears the crown.

Then he gave a shrill piercing whistle and the bird flew down and perched on his arm, with sharp beak pressed against him.

Timothy stared, both at the wondrous beauty of the bird and the strange appearance of the old man.

"You be looking for holly berries?" asked the man.

"Yes, sir," replied Timothy.

"Your bird seems to have a liking for them, for I've found never an odd berry in all these woods."

"They are his food. They belong to him, from time immemorial."

"I've never seen such a bird before," said Timothy.

"No, and you wouldn't have seen him today if it hadn't been Christmas Eve,

59

and the moon young, and the star in the sky."

Timothy looked up and in the green-blue sky in the west he saw the thin young crescent moon and one bright star.

"If you want some berries, I will give you some, for you'll not find any by yourself this year. It is only once in a hundred years we come for them.

Timothy could well believe it, for the man looked so old he might have been one of the ancient trees come to life.

"I'll give you some berries better than any others," said the man, stepping back to the great holly tree, and the bird balanced on his arm and fluttered its lovely wings.

The old man reached up to the holly tree, and drew down a branch which had three berries growing on it. Timothy hadn't seen them, but they shone like burning fire in the glossy leaves.

"Three holly berries. One for you and one for your wife and one for the babe in the cradle," said the old man, holding out the branch to Timothy.

"How did you know I have a wife and baby?" asked Timothy astonished.

"I can read men's minds," said the ancient man, and he stroked the bright feathers of the bird, and laid his withered cheek on the soft wings. "I know you are Timothy Snow, and your father was Timothy Snow, killed by a falling tree, and your son is Timothy also. I could tell you other things, but that is enough."

"Who are you?" asked Timothy. "You're a stranger in these parts surely, for I've lived here for all my twenty years, and never set eyes on you before. Are you shepherd at one of the hill farms away yonder? They have an old man working there."

"I'm a shepherd from over the hills, from a distant land. I'm a shepherd wandering the earth, returning at Christmas for a brief visit to my flocks of green trees."

"And what may you be called?" asked Timothy.

"Holly is my name. Old Holly, once young Holly, and that was when King Henry was on the throne. My father was Old Holly, too."

"And the bird?" asked Timothy, and he stretched out a hand to touch the bird's feathers. Quickly he drew back, for they were sharp as thorns. Then he saw that every feather was like a holly leaf with pointed edge upturned.

"He is a Holly Bird," said the old man. "He lives with me in the heart of the unseen world. And now I will bid you good day, and may good fortune favour you this Christmas."

"A happy Christmas to you, Old Holly, sir," called Timothy. The old man moved slowly away under the drooping boughs of the great holly trees. The branches dipped to the earth, and as the old man walked under he disappeared as completely as if he had stepped into the hearts of the trees. Timothy lifted the leaves and stepped after him, but the beautiful bird and the old man had gone. There was no sign or shadow, only a green feather lay there, pricked and jagged like a holly leaf.

So Timothy put the holly bough with the three scarlet berries on his shoulder and started off towards home. Only three berries for Jenny Wren, and for little Timothy, but what a tale he had to tell! He would tell it over and over again, with details of the old man's coat and long boots, and fleece like snow and eyes bright as stars in the wrinkled face, and the bird with its barbed feathers and its topaz eyes and its crest of gold. Jenny Wren would open her brown eyes and

gaze at him, but she would understand something that was hidden, an unknown mystery. So back he went to the cottage. It was dark when Timothy reached home, but Jenny Wren had lighted the lamp and left the shutters unclosed, so that a gold beam streamed over the field to meet him. His heart was warmed as he trudged towards that beam of joy where little Timothy lay snug in his cradle.

He had been farther into the woods than he realized, he had walked many miles and there was only the holly branch to show. As he walked up the garden path the door was flung open and Jenny Wren rushed out and threw her arms around him.

"Oh, Timothy. I thought you were lost," she cried, burying her face in his thick coat. "Where have you been all day, and where's the holly?"

"Jenny my love, this is all I've brought – three holly berries!" said he sadly.

"Three holly berries," echoed Jenny, taking the glistening bough of dark leaves with their three jewels of berries. "Only this after a day in the woods!"

"Never mind," she added quickly when Timothy's face fell. "There's one for me and one for you and one for baby Timothy."

"That's what Old Holly said when he gave me the bough," said Timothy. "I'll tell you my tale while I have supper. Then we'll hang up our decorations, for I've walked many a mile and I'm tired."

So Timothy ate his Christmas Eve supper of green sage-cheese and mince pies and hot posset, which he drank in the two-handled posset mug, and as he ate and drank he told the tale of the woods, of the ancient man, whose name was Holly, and the bright Holly bird which flitted through the trees. Jenny sat with her arms on the table, listening wide-eyed to her husband.

"Well, it is certainly a lovely bit of holly! Even if there are only three berries to decorate our room, they are the best I've ever seen, and the leaves glitter like polished brass," said Jenny, when her husband had finished. "He must have been one of those folk of other days you hear of sometimes, come back to earth. Well, I've got some streamers of ivy and some yew and bay. We will make a kissing-bunch and put those berries in it. Then everyone who comes will see them."

So they decorated the kitchen, and strung the sprays of ivy round the coloured almanacks on the wall, and put yew over the grandfather clock in the corner, and branches of smooth sweet-smelling bay among the shining saucepans on the shelf. The holly they twisted in a round bunch, with a couple of flags and a glass bell and apples and oranges on it, and that was the kissing-bunch. They hung it from the hook in the middle of the low ceiling, and then they kissed one another beneath it.

Whether it was the candlelight, or the flickering fire, or the ardour of their kisses I do not know, but those three holly berries shone like scarlet flames. They glowed with a light of their own which put the candles to shame, and the little room seemed to be full of dancing shadows and flickering points of flame, coming from the three lovely holly berries in the kissing-bunch.

Even when Timothy blew out the candles to save the candle-wax and sat in the dusky light, the berries shone and every leaf of holly sent out a gleam like a star. There was a sweet fragrance in the air, and a soft ringing of bells, but when Jenny asked Timothy if he noticed these things he said the sweetness was from Jenny Wren's brown hair, and the ringing of the bells was in their hearts.

"Nay! I'm sure there is a far-away bell ringing," said Jenny, as she sat in the firelight and held Timothy's hand.

She watched the shadows moving on the wall, and as she looked she saw an age-old story, for out of the darkness came three men, hooded figures, who moved across the room and hovered near the cradle, bending low to it, holding out their long, thin hands with gifts.

"Look! Look! The Three Wise Men," she whispered awe-struck, but Timothy's eyes were shut, he was fast asleep after the long walk. Only the mother saw the vision of the East.

The three shadows knelt there, and others came crowding round, men with shepherds' crooks in their hands. Soft bells rang more clearly and the sweetness in the little room was like incense. Then the shadows arose and went their way, moving across the whitewashed wall and fading in the firelight.

Christmas Day was the happiest Timothy could remember, and Jenny Wren agreed with him that never had she felt such bliss as filled her heart. They were too far from a church to go there with the baby, but they sang their Christmas hymn together and said their Christmas prayer. Timothy gave Jenny a little silver locket which he had bought in the town when he went to sell his wood, and Jenny gave Timothy the thick white stockings and scarf which she had knitted for him and embroidered with scarlet holly berries and leaves. Then little Timothy received his presents, a lamb carved from a piece of white holly wood, which Big Timothy had made secretly, whittling it with his knife when he had his dinner among the trees. Jenny gave her little son a pair of tiny white slippers, woven from sheep's wool, tied with red ribbons.

The baby crowed and laughed over his presents, but he stretched up his hand to the kissing-bunch. He leapt in Timothy's arms when he was held up to see the silvery bell and shining ball of glass.

"It's the berries he's after. Look, Timothy. Look how bright they are!" cried Jenny.

The holly berries glowed like three fires in the kissing-bunch. They seemed larger and finer even than the night before, and they flamed as if a hidden beacon were there. Both Timothy and Jenny stared at them in silence, and little Timothy leapt and crowed and chuckled with tiny fat hands upraised to them.

"Let him have them," said Timothy. "See, I'll pick them off, and hold them in my hand for him to look at."

He gathered the three berries and held them in the palm of his hand. Jenny stopped over them, breathing the exquisite smell which came from them. The baby was forgotten, for the berries were expanding as they slowly opened.

The scarlet skins cracked asunder, and the sweet fragrance filled the room.

It curled up like blue smoke, and hung in the shape of a holly tree with pointed leaves and a crown of thorns on the top. The berries dropped apart, with skin back-turned to show their hidden treasures. In one lay a bag of gold dust. In another a casket of frankincense. In the third a pot of sweet myrrh.

"Gold, frankincense and myrrh," murmured Jenny. "In memory of the first Christmas Day, Timothy."

Jenny put the miracles away in the oak chest, each wrapped in the scarlet skin of its berry. They were gifts for their little child. The past was to be a present to bring hope for the future.

Every Christmas Timothy told the tale of the strange happenings in the deep wood, and Jenny showed the beautiful gifts to little Timothy. Sometimes father and son walked through the woods seeking the trees where Old Holly had waited with the flaming bird on his arm, but they never saw him again.

The Wicked Singers

KIT WRIGHT

And have you been out carol singing,
Collecting for the Old Folk's Dinner?

Oh yes indeed, oh yes indeed.

And did you sing all the Christmas numbers,
Every one a winner?

Oh yes indeed, oh yes indeed.

Good King Wenceslas, and Hark
The Herald Angels Sing?

Oh yes indeed, oh yes indeed.

And did you sing them loud and clear
And make the night sky ring?

Oh yes indeed, oh yes indeed.

And did you count up all the money?
Was it quite a lot?

Oh yes indeed, oh yes indeed.

And did you give it all to the Vicar,
Everything you'd got?

Certainly not, certainly not.

Mice in the Hay

LESLIE NORRIS

out of the lamplight
whispering worshipping
the mice in the hay

timid eyes pearl-bright
whispering worshipping
whisking quick and away

they were there that night
whispering worshipping
smaller than snowflakes are

quietly made their way
whispering worshipping
close to the manger

yes, they were afraid
whispering worshipping
as the journey was made

from a dark corner
whispering worshipping
scuttling together

But He smiled to see them
whispering worshipping
there in the lamplight

stretched out His hand to them
they saw the baby King
hurried back out of sight
whispering worshipping

Christmas Eve

SANDY BROWNJOHN

Our mother was tearing her hair out,
(My sister and I played upstairs),
There was too much to do,
She would never be through,
And the air was quite blue;
So father had made himself scarce.

He'd been sent to do last-minute shopping
With a list as long as your arm.
Then to us mother said,
"You be useful instead,
Go and clear up the shed —
And leave me some peace to get calm!"

We put on our coats and our wellies
And moaned as we went through the door.
The thick cloud hung low,
And its strange, muddy glow
Held the promise of snow,
And the wind was quite biting and raw.

Our shed wasn't much of a building —
Its door had come off long ago.
What was once a tool-store
Now had cobwebs galore,
Fieldmice under the floor,
And corners where fungus could grow.

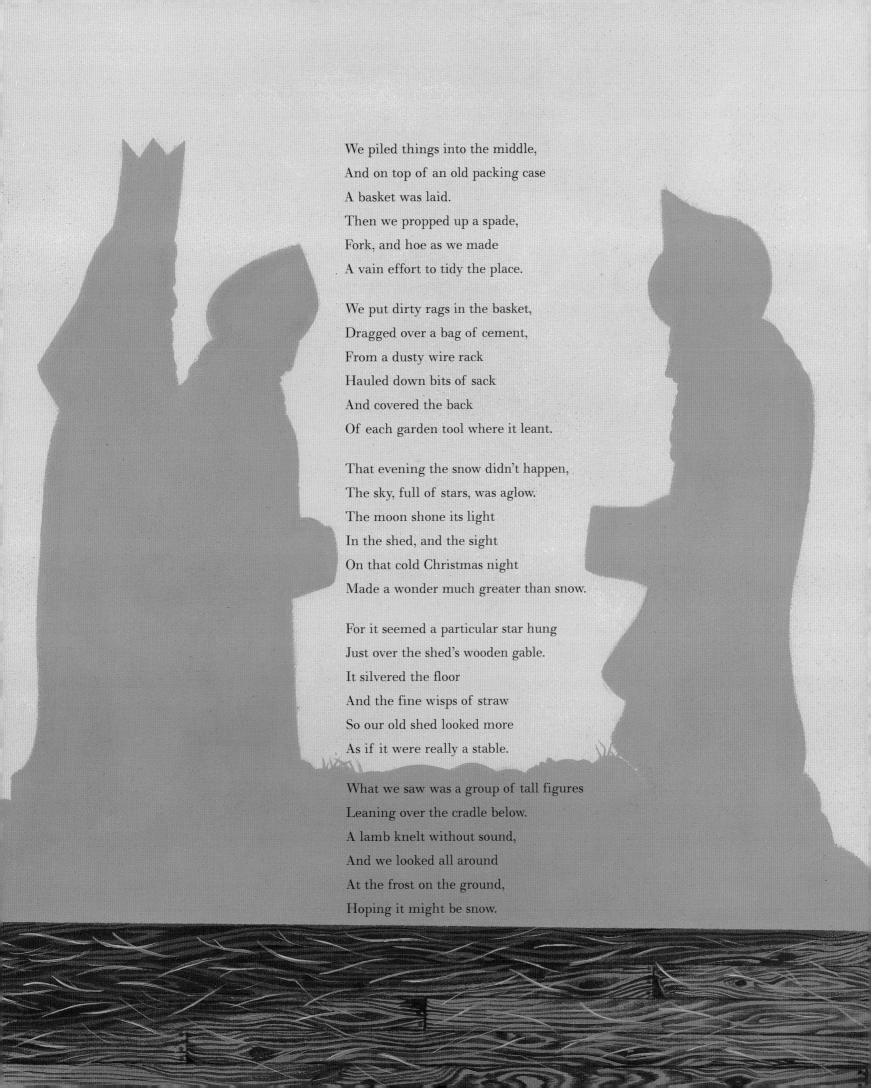

We piled things into the middle,
And on top of an old packing case
A basket was laid.
Then we propped up a spade,
Fork, and hoe as we made
A vain effort to tidy the place.

We put dirty rags in the basket,
Dragged over a bag of cement,
From a dusty wire rack
Hauled down bits of sack
And covered the back
Of each garden tool where it leant.

That evening the snow didn't happen,
The sky, full of stars, was aglow.
The moon shone its light
In the shed, and the sight
On that cold Christmas night
Made a wonder much greater than snow.

For it seemed a particular star hung
Just over the shed's wooden gable.
It silvered the floor
And the fine wisps of straw
So our old shed looked more
As if it were really a stable.

What we saw was a group of tall figures
Leaning over the cradle below.
A lamb knelt without sound,
And we looked all around
At the frost on the ground,
Hoping it might be snow.

Merry Christmas

AILEEN FISHER

I saw on the snow
when I tried my skis
the track of a mouse
beside some trees.

Before he tunnelled
to reach his house
he wrote "Merry Christmas"
in white, in mouse.

We Three Kings of Orient Are

JOHN HENRY HOPKINS

We three kings of Orient are;
Bearing gifts we traverse afar,
Field and fountain, moor and mountain,
Following yonder star.

O star of wonder, star of night,
Star with royal beauty bright,
Westward leading, still proceeding,
Guide us to thy perfect light.

Melchior:

Born a king on Bethlehem plain,
Gold I bring, to crown him again,
King forever, ceasing never,
Over us all to reign.

Caspar:

Frankincense to offer have I,
Incense owns a deity nigh;
Prayer and praising, all men raising,
Worship him, God most high.

Balthazar:

Myrrh is mine; its bitter perfume
Breathes a life of gathering gloom;
Sorrowing, sighing, bleeding, dying,
Sealed in the stone-cold tomb.

Glorious now behold him arise,
King and God and sacrifice,
Alleluia, alleluia,
Earth to the heavens replies.

73

Christmas Card

TED HUGHES

You have anti-freeze in the car, yes,
      But the shivering stars wade deeper.
Your scarf's tucked in under your buttons,
      But a dry snow ticks through the stubble.
Your knee-boots gleam in the fashion,
      But the moon must stay

        And stamp and cry
        As the holly the holly
        Hots its reds

Electric blanket to comfort your bedtime
      The river no longer feels its stones.
Your windows are steamed by dumpling laughter
      The snowplough's buried on the drifted moor.
Carols shake your television
      And nothing moves on the road but the wind

        Hither and thither
        The wind and three
        Starving sheep.

Redwings from Norway rattle at the clouds

      But comfortless sneezers puddle in pubs.

The robin looks in at the kitchen window

      But all care huddles to hearths and kettles.

The sun lobs one wet snowball feebly

      Grim and blue

            The dusk of the coombe

            And the swamp woodland

            Sinks with the wren.

See old lips go purple and old brows go paler.

      The stiff crow drops in the midnight silence.

Sneezes grow coughs and coughs grow painful.

      The vixen yells in the midnight garden.

You wake with the shakes and watch your breathing

      Smoke in the moonlight – silent, silent

            Your anklebone

            And your anklebone

            Lie big in the bed.

Winter Night

EDNA ST VINCENT MILLAY

Pile high the hickory and the light
Log of chestnut struck by the blight.
Welcome in the winter night.

The day has gone in hewing and felling,
Sawing and drawing wood to the dwelling
For the night of talk and story-telling.

These are the hours that give the edge
To the blunted axe and the bent wedge,
Straighten the saw and lighten the sledge.

Here are question and reply,
And the fire reflected in the thinking eye.
So peace, and let the bob-cat cry.

Questions on Christmas Eve

WES MAGEE

But *how* can his reindeer fly without wings?
Jets on their hooves? That's plain cheating!
And *how* can he climb down the chimney pot
　When we've got central heating?

You say it's all magic and I shouldn't ask
About Santa on Christmas Eve.
But I'm confused by the stories I've heard;
　I don't know what to believe.

I said that I'd sit up in bed all night long
To see if he really would call.
But I fell fast asleep, woke up after dawn
　As something banged in the hall.

I saw my sock crammed with apples and sweets;
There were parcels piled high near the door.
Jingle bells tinkled far off in the dark;
　One snowflake shone on the floor.

The Goose is Getting Fat

MICHAEL MORPURGO

Gertrude was a goose like any other goose. Hatched out in the orchard one grizzly morning in June, she spent those early weeks looking at the world from the warm sanctuary of her mother's all-enveloping softness. It might have come as a surprise to her to know that her mother was not a goose. Of course Gertrude was convinced she was, and that was all that mattered; but in reality mother was a rather ragged speckled hen. She was, however, the most pugnacious, the most jealous and possessive hen on the farm, and that was why Charlie's father had shut her up inside a coop with a vast goose egg and kept her there until something happened. Each day she had been lifted off and the egg sprinkled with water to soften the shell. The summer had been dry that year, and all the early clutches of goose eggs had failed. This was very probably the last chance they had of rearing a goose for Christmas.

There had always been a goose for Christmas Day, Charlie's father said — a goose reared on their own corn and in their own orchard. So he had picked out the nastiest, broodiest hen in the yard to guard the egg and to rear his Christmas goose, and Charlie had sprinkled the egg each day.

When Charlie and his father first spied the golden gosling scavenging in the long grass with the speckled black hen clucking close by, they raced each other up the lane to break the good news to Charlie's mother. She pretended to be as happy about it all as they were, but in her heart of hearts she had been hoping that there would be no goose to rear and pluck that year. The job she detested most was fattening the goose for Christmas and then plucking it. The plucking took her hours, and the feathers flew everywhere, clouds of them – in her hair, down her neck. Her wrists and fingers ached with the work of it. But worst of all, she could not bear to look at the sweet, sad face she had come to know so well, hanging down over her knee, still smiling. She would willingly pluck a pheasant, a hen, even a woodcock; she would skin and gut a rabbit – anything but another goose.

Now Charlie's father was no fool and he knew his wife well enough to sense her disappointment. It was to soften the news, to console her and no doubt to persuade her again, that he suggested that Charlie might help this year. He had his arm round Charlie's shoulder, and that always made Charlie feel like a man.

"Charlie's almost ten now, lovely," he said. Charlie's father always called his mother "lovely", and Charlie liked that. "Ten years old next January, and he'll be as tall as you next Christmas. He'll be taller than me before he's through growing. Just look at him, he's grown an inch since breakfast."

"I know Charlie's nearly ten, dear," she said. "I was there when he was born, remember?"

"Course you were, my lovely," Charlie's father said,

taking the drying-up cloth from her and sitting down at the kitchen table. "I've got a plan, see. I known you've never been keen on rearing the goose for Christmas, and Charlie and me have been thinking about it, haven't we, Charlie?" Charlie hadn't a clue what his father was talking about, but he grinned and nodded anyway because it seemed the best thing to do. "We thought that this year all three of us could look after the goose, you know, together like. Charlie boy can feed her up each day and drive her in each night. He can fatten her up for us. I'll kill her when the time comes – I know it seems a terrible thing to do, but that's got to be done has got to be done – and perhaps you wouldn't mind doing the little bit of plucking at the end for us. How would that be, my lovely?"

Charlie was flattered by the confidence his father had placed in him and his mother was, as usual, beguiled by both his Welsh tongue and the warmth of his smile. And so it was that Charlie came to rear the Christmas goose.

The fluffy, flippered gosling was soon exploring every part of the orchard and soon outgrew her bad-tempered foster mother. The hen shadowed her for as long as she could. Then she gave up and went back to the farmyard. The gosling turned into a goose, long and lovely and white. Charlie watched her grow. He would feed her twice a day, before and after school, with a little mixed corn. On fine autumn days he would sit with her in the orchard for hours at a time and watch her grazing under the trees. And he loved to watch her preening herself, her eyes closed in ecstasy as she curved her long neck and delved into the white feathers on her chest.

Charlie called the goose "Gertrude" because she reminded him of his tall, lean Aunty Gertrude who always wore feathers in her hat in church. His aunt's nose was so imperial in shape and size that her neck seemed permanently stretched with the effort of seeing over it. But she was, for all that, immensely elegant and poised, so there could be no other name for the goose but Gertrude. And Gertrude moved through her orchard kingdom with an air of haughty indifference and an easy elegance that sets a goose apart from all other fowl. To Charlie, however, Gertrude had more than this. She had the gentle charm and sweetness of nature that Charlie warmed to as the autumn months passed.

They harvested cider apples in late October, so Gertrude's peace was disturbed each day for over two weeks as they climbed the lichen-coated apple trees and shook until the apples rained down on the grass. Gertrude and Charlie stood side by side waiting for the storm to pass, and then Charlie moved in to gather up the apples and fill the sacks. Gertrude stood back like a foreman and cackled encouragement from a distance. Her wings were fully grown now, and in her excitement she would raise herself to her full height, open her great white wings, stretch her neck, and beat the air with wild enthusiasm.

"It's clapping, she is," said Charlie's father from high up in the tree. "A grand bird. She's growing well. Be fine by Christmas if you look after her. We've got plenty of Bramley apples this year, good for stuffing. Nothing like apple stuffing in a Christmas goose, is there, Charlie?"

The words fell like stones on Charlie's heart. As a farmer's son he knew that most of the animals on the farm went for slaughter. It was an accepted fact of life; neither a cause for sorrow nor rejoicing. Sick lambs, rescued piglets, ill suckling calves – Charlie helped

to care for all of them and had already developed that degree of detachment that a farmer needs unless he is to be on the phone to the vet five times a day. But none of these animals were killed on the farm — they went away to be killed, and so he did not have to think about it. Charlie had seen his father shoot rats and pigeons and squirrels; but that again was different, they were pests.

Now, for the first time, as he watched Gertrude patrolling behind the dung heap, he realized that she had only two months to live, that she would be killed, hung up, plucked, pulled, stuffed and cooked, and borne in triumph onto the table on Christmas Day. "Nothing like apple stuffing in a Christmas goose," — his father's words would not go away.

Gertrude lowered her head and hissed at an intruding gaggle of hens that flew up in a panic and scattered into the hedgerow. She raised her wings again and beat them in a dazzling display before resuming her dignified patrol. She was magnificent, Charlie thought, a queen among geese. At that moment he decided that Gertrude was not going to be killed for Christmas. He would simply not allow it to happen.

With frosts and winds of November the last of the leaves were blown from the trees and swirled round the farmyard. Then the winter rains came and piled them into soggy mushy heaps against the hedgerows, clogging the ditches and filling the pot-holes. It was fine weather for a goose, though, and Gertrude revelled in the wildness of the winter winds. She stalked serenely through the leaves, her head held high against the wind and the rain, her feathers blown and ruffled.

Each day when Charlie got back from school he drove Gertrude in from the orchard to the safety of an empty calf pen. Foxes do come out on windy nights, and he did not want Gertrude taken by the fox any more than he wanted her carved up at Christmas. Before breakfast every morning Charlie opened the calf pen, and the two of them walked side by side out into the orchard where he emptied the scoop of corn into Gertrude's bowl. He talked to her all the while of the great master-plan he had dreamed up and how she must learn not to cackle too loudly.

"Won't be long now, Gerty," he said. "But if you make too much noise, you're done for. Your goose will be cooked, and that's for sure." But Gerty wasn't listening. She had found a leafy puddle and was busy drinking from it, dipping and lifting her head, dipping and lifting…

Until late November his father had not taken much interest in Gertrude's progress, but now with Christmas only six weeks away he was asking almost daily whether or not Gertrude would be fat enough in time. "She'll do better on oats, Charlie," he said one breakfast. "And I think you ought to shut her up now, and I don't mean just at night. I mean all the time. This wandering about in the orchard is all very well, but she won't put on much weight that way. There won't be much left on her for us, will there? You leave her in the calf pen from now on and feed her up."

"She wouldn't like that," Charlie said. "You know she wouldn't. She likes her freedom. She'd pine away inside and lose weight." Charlie had his reasons for wanting to keep Gertrude out in the orchard by day.

"Charlie's right, dear," his mother said softly. "Of course you're both right, really." His mother was a perfect diplomat. "Gertrude will fatten up better inside, but its lean meat we want, no fat. The more natural food she eats and the happier she is, the better she'll taste. My father used to say, 'A happy goose is a tender goose.' And anyway, there's only the three of us on Christmas Day, and Aunt Gertrude, of course. What would we do with a fifteen-pound goose?"

"All right, my lovely," said Charlie's father. "I know better than to argue when you and Charlie get together. But feed her on oats, Charlie, else there'll be nothing on her but skin and bone. And remember I have to kill her about a week before Christmas — a goose needs a few days to hang. And then you'll need a day or so for plucking and dressing, won't you, lovely? I can smell it already," he said, closing his eyes and sniffing the air. "Goose and apple stuffing, roast potatoes, sprouts and chipolata sausages. Oh, Christmas is coming and the goose is getting fat!"

The days rolled by into December, and Christmas beckoned. There was a Nativity play at school in which Charlie played Joseph. There was the endless shopping expeditions into town when Charlie dragged along behind his mother, who would never make up her mind about anything. Christmas with all its heady excitement meant little to Charlie that year for all he could think of was Gertrude. Again and again he went over the rescue plan in his mind until he was sure he had left nothing to chance.

December 16th was the day Charlie decided upon. It was a Saturday, so he would be home all day.

But more important, that morning, Charlie knew his father would be out following the hunt five miles away at Dolton. He had asked Charlie if he wanted to go with him, but Charlie said he had to clean out Gertrude's pen. "It's a pity you can't come," said his father. "Lovely frosty morning. There'll be a fine scent."

Charlie watched from the farm gate until his father rattled off down the lane in the battered Land Rover. Then Charlie wasted no time. It was a long walk down to the river and he had to make a detour through the woods out of sight in case his mother spotted him.

Gertrude was waiting by the door of the calf pen as usual, impatient to get out into the orchard. But this morning she was not allowed to stop by her bowl of corn. Instead she was driven firmly out into the field beyond the orchard. She protested noisily, cackling and hissing, trying to get back by turning this way and that. But Charlie paid no attention. He banged his stick on the ground to keep her moving on. "It's for your own good, Gerty, you'll see," he said. "It has to be far away to be safe. It's a hiding place no one will ever find. No one goes there in the winter, Gerty. You'll be as safe as houses down there, and no one will eat you for Christmas. Next year you'll be too tough to eat anyway. They say a goose can live for forty years. Think of that – not six months but forty years. So stop making a fuss, and walk on."

He talked to her all the way down through Watercress Field, into Little Wood and out into Lower Down. By the time they reached the Marsh, Gertrude was exhausted and had stopped her cackling. Every gateway was a trial, with the puddles iced over. Try as she did, the goose could not keep her balance. She slithered and slipped across the ice until she found the ground rough and hard under her feet again. All the while the stick beat the ground behind her so that she could not turn around and go home. The fishing hut stood only a few yards from the river, an ugly building, squat and corrugated, but ideal for housing a refugee goose.

In the last few days Charlie had moved out all the fishing tackle. He had laid a thick carpet of straw on the floor so that Gertrude would be warm and comfortable.

In one corner was the old hip bath he had found in the attic. The bath was brim full of water and Charlie had hitched a ramp over the side. By the door was a feeding trough already full of corn. But Gertrude was not impressed by her new home. She walked straight to the darkest end of the hut and hissed angrily at Charlie. He rattled the trough to show her where the corn was, but the goose looked away disdainfully. Her whole routine had been rudely disturbed and all she wanted to do was to sulk.

"You'll be all right, Gerty," said Charlie. "But if you do hear anyone, don't start cackling. You've got food and water, and I'll be down to see you when I can. I can't come too often. It's a long way and they might get suspicious." Gertrude hissed at him once again and turned her head away. "I love you too!" said Charlie, and he went out bolting the door firmly behind him.

Charlie ran back all the way home because he needed to be breathless when he got there. His mother was just finishing icing the cake when Charlie came bursting in through the kitchen door. "She's gone. Gertrude's gone. She's not in the orchard. She's not anywhere."

Charlie and his mother searched all that morning and through the afternoon until the frost came down with the darkness and forced them to stop. Of course they found no sign of Gertrude.

"I can't understand it," said Charlie's mother, as they broke the news to his father. "She's just vanished. There's no feathers and no blood."

"Well I can't believe it's a fox, anyway," said Charlie's father. "Not in broad daylight with a hunt just on the other side of the parish. She's in a hedge somewhere, laying an egg perhaps. They do that in winter sometimes, you know. She'll be back as soon as she gets hungry. It's a pity, though. She'll lose weight out in the cold."

Charlie's mother was upset. "We'll never find her if it snows. They've forecast snow tonight."

And that night the snow did come. Snow upon snow. When Charlie looked out of his bedroom window the next morning, the farm had been transformed. Every muddy lane and rusty roof was immaculate with snow. Charlie was out early, as usual, helping his father feed the bullocks before breakfast. Then, saying he wanted to look for Gertrude, he set off towards the river, carrying a bucket of corn.

Gertrude hissed as he opened the door of the fishing hut, but when she saw who it was, she broke into an excited cackle and opened her wings in pure delight. She loved Charlie again. Charlie poured out the corn and topped up the water in the hip bath. "So far, so good, Gerty," he said. "Not so bad in here, is it?" Better in here than out.

There's snow outside, but you'll be warm enough in here. Father thinks you're laying an egg in a hedge somewhere. Mother's worried sick about you. I can't tell her until after Christmas, though, 'cos she'd have to tell father. But she'll understand, and she'll make father understand, too. See you tomorrow, Gerty."

Every day for a week, Charlie trudged down through the snow to feed Gertrude. By this time both his mother and father had given up all hope of ever finding their Christmas goose. "It must have been a fox," his mother reflected sadly. "Gerty wouldn't just have walked off. But you'd think there would have been a tell-tale feather or two, wouldn't you? Don't be upset, Charlie."

Charlie had always found it easy to bring tears to his eyes and he did so now. "But she was my goose," he sniffed. "It was all my fault. I should have shut her up like father said."

"Come on, Charlie," said his father, putting an arm round him. "We can't have all these tears over a goose, now can we? After all we were going to eat her, and have you ever heard of anyone crying over Christmas dinner?"

Charlie was proud of his tearful performance, but was careful not to overdo it. "I'll be all right," he said manfully. "I'm going to keep looking, though, just in case."

One night, two days before Christmas, the wind changed from the north-east and rain came in from the west. By the morning, the snow had gone and the farm looked real and untidy again. Charlie could see the brook from his window. But instead of a gentle burbling stream, the brook had turned into a raging brown torrent rushing down towards the river. The river!

89

If the river burst its bank the fishing hut would be under water, Gertrude would be trapped inside. She wasn't used to swimming. Her feathers would be waterlogged and she would drown.

He dressed quickly and within minutes was running down towards the river. As he opened the gate into the marsh, he could see that the hut was completely surrounded by water and that the door was wide open. He splashed through the floods, praying that he would find Gertrude still alive and safe. But Gertrude wasn't even there. The trough and the straw floated in a foot of muddy water, but of Gertrude there was neither sound nor sight.

Somehow the door had opened and Gerty had escaped. He must have forgotten to bolt it, and the force of the flood water had done the rest. Now Gertrude was out there somewhere in the floods on her own. This time she had really escaped and when Charlie cried he really meant it, and the tears flowed uncontrollably.

Charlie spent the rest of the day searching the banks of the river for Gertrude, calling everywhere for her. But it was no use. The river was still high and flowing fast. He could only think that she had been swept away in the floods and drowned. He was filled with a sense of hopeless despair and wretchedness. He longed to tell his mother, but of course he could not. He dared not even show his feelings.

In the evening Aunty Gertrude arrived, for it was Christmas Eve. A tree was brought in and together they decorated it before joining the carol singers in the village. But Charlie's heart was not in any of it. He went to bed and fell asleep without even putting his stocking out.

But when he awoke on Christmas morning the first thing he noticed was his stocking standing stiff as a sentry by his bedside table. Intrigued and suddenly excited, he felt to see what was inside the stocking. All he found was a tangerine and a piece of long, stiff card. He pulled out the card and looked at it. On it was written:

To Charlie, from Father Christmas:
Goosey Goosey Gander, where shall I wander?
From the orchard to the fishing hut,
From the fishing hut to the hay-barn …

It was clearly his mother's handwriting.

Charlie tiptoed downstairs in his dressing-gown, slipped on his wellingtons and then ran out across the back yard to the hay-barn. He unlatched the little wooden door and stepped inside. In the farthest corner, penned up against a wall of hay were two tall geese that cackled and hissed at his approach. They sidled away together into the hay, their heads almost touching. Charlie crept closer. One was a splendid grey goose he had never seen before. But the other looked distinctly familiar. And when she stretched out her white wings, there could be no doubt that this was Gertrude.

But his attention was drawn to a beautifully decorated card which read:

To Dearest Charlie from Gertrude, I've got a message from your mother and father. Your mother says you should remember that if you walk in snow you leave footprints that can be followed. And you father says: Nice try, Charlie boy. We're having chicken for lunch today. Aunty Gertrude likes it better, anyway.

Look after the geese. You'd better. They're yours for keeps!

So Charlie, meet Berty – he's a gander. He's my husband, Charlie, a present from Father Christmas, and I hope you like him as much as I do. Oh, and by the way, thanks for saving my neck. I couldn't have asked for a better friend.

Much love for Christmas,

Gerty

By the time Charlie got back to the house, everyone was sitting down in the kitchen and having breakfast. Aunty Gertrude wished him a Happy Christmas and asked him what he'd had in his stocking. "A goose, Aunty," he said, smiling. "And a tangerine!"

Charlie looked at his mother and then at his father. Both were trying hard not to laugh. "Happy Christmas, Charlie boy, any sign of Gertrude yet?" his father asked.

"Yes," said Charlie, swallowing his excitement. "Father Christmas found her and brought her back – and Berty too – her husband, you know. Nice of him, wasn't it?"

"Gertrude?" said Aunt Gertrude, looking bewildered. "A goose in your stocking?" She looked over her nose just like a certain goose. "I don't understand. What's this all about?"

"Later, dear," said Charlie's mother, gently patting her sister's arm. "I'll tell you about it later, after we've eaten our Christmas dinner!"

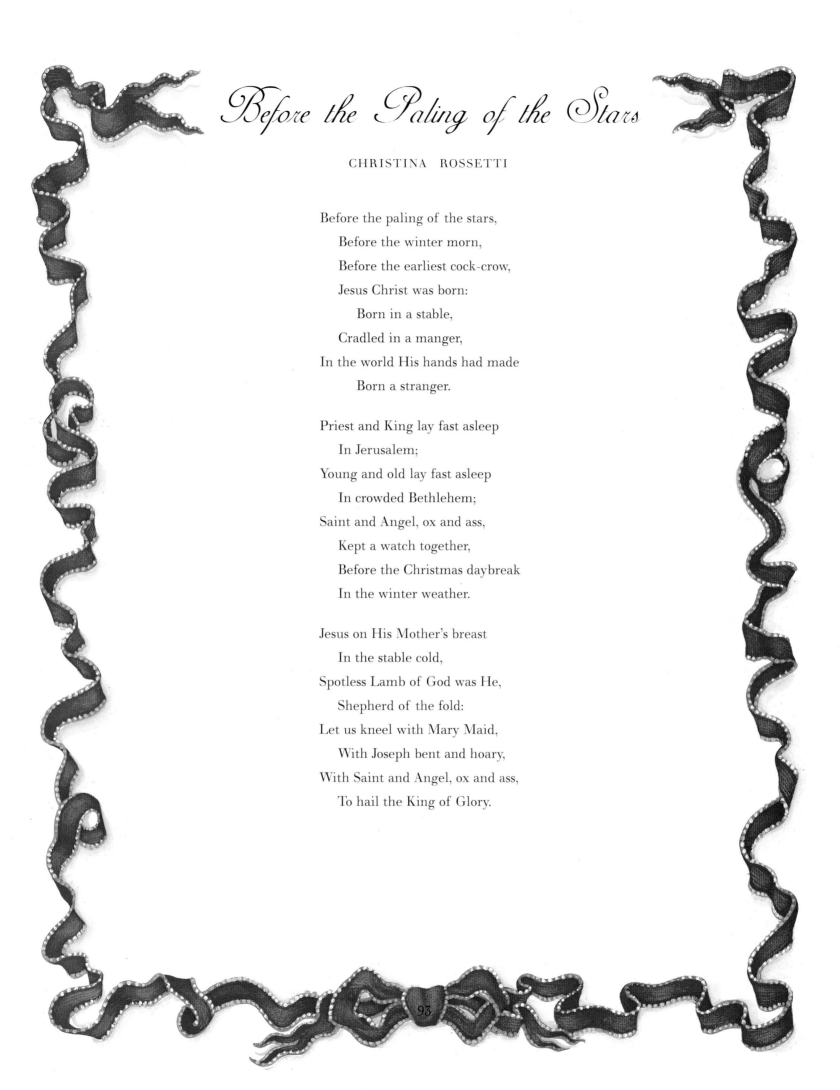

Before the Paling of the Stars

CHRISTINA ROSSETTI

Before the paling of the stars,
    Before the winter morn,
    Before the earliest cock-crow,
    Jesus Christ was born:
        Born in a stable,
    Cradled in a manger,
In the world His hands had made
        Born a stranger.

Priest and King lay fast asleep
    In Jerusalem;
Young and old lay fast asleep
    In crowded Bethlehem;
Saint and Angel, ox and ass,
    Kept a watch together,
    Before the Christmas daybreak
    In the winter weather.

Jesus on His Mother's breast
    In the stable cold,
Spotless Lamb of God was He,
    Shepherd of the fold:
Let us kneel with Mary Maid,
    With Joseph bent and hoary,
With Saint and Angel, ox and ass,
    To hail the King of Glory.

Index

TITLES & AUTHORS

FIRST LINES

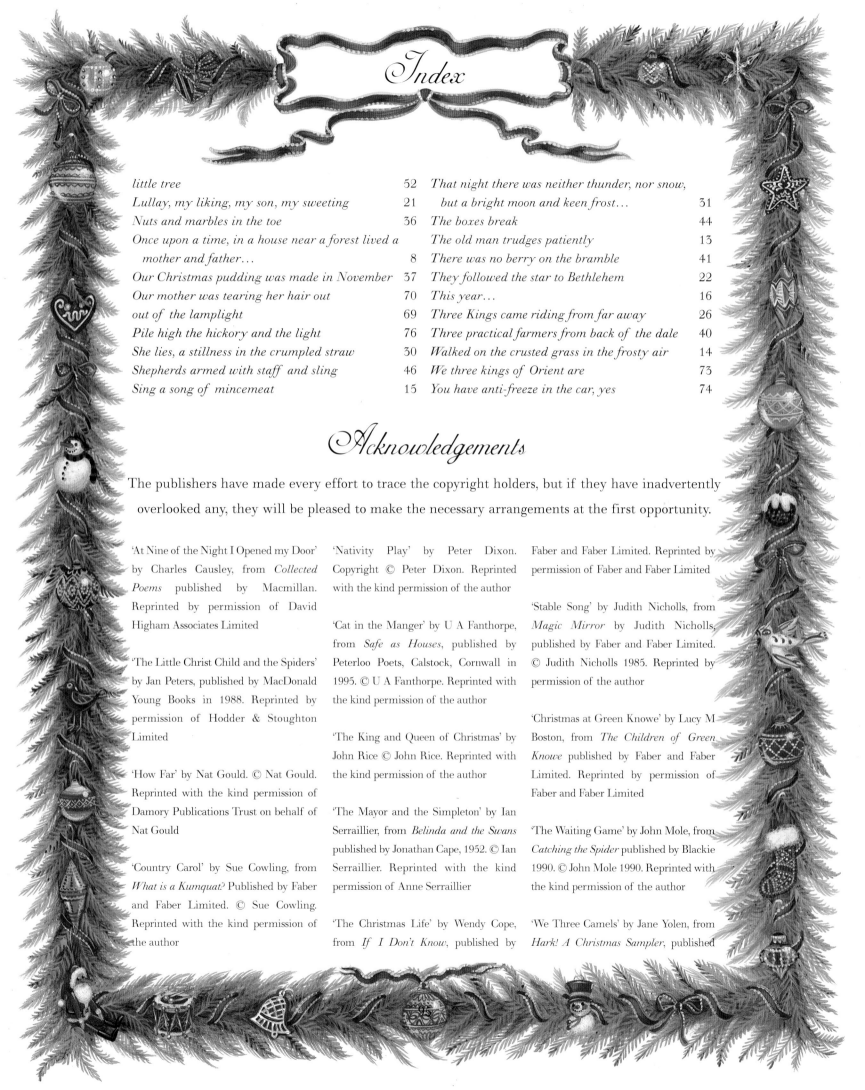

Index

Acknowledgements

The publishers have made every effort to trace the copyright holders, but if they have inadvertently overlooked any, they will be pleased to make the necessary arrangements at the first opportunity.

'At Nine of the Night I Opened my Door' by Charles Causley, from *Collected Poems* published by Macmillan. Reprinted by permission of David Higham Associates Limited

'The Little Christ Child and the Spiders' by Jan Peters, published by MacDonald Young Books in 1988. Reprinted by permission of Hodder & Stoughton Limited

'How Far' by Nat Gould. © Nat Gould. Reprinted with the kind permission of Damory Publications Trust on behalf of Nat Gould

'Country Carol' by Sue Cowling, from *What is a Kumquat?* Published by Faber and Faber Limited. © Sue Cowling. Reprinted with the kind permission of the author

'Nativity Play' by Peter Dixon. Copyright © Peter Dixon. Reprinted with the kind permission of the author

'Cat in the Manger' by U A Fanthorpe, from *Safe as Houses*, published by Peterloo Poets, Calstock, Cornwall in 1995. © U A Fanthorpe. Reprinted with the kind permission of the author

'The King and Queen of Christmas' by John Rice © John Rice. Reprinted with the kind permission of the author

'The Mayor and the Simpleton' by Ian Serraillier, from *Belinda and the Swans* published by Jonathan Cape, 1952. © Ian Serraillier. Reprinted with the kind permission of Anne Serraillier

'The Christmas Life' by Wendy Cope, from *If I Don't Know*, published by

Faber and Faber Limited. Reprinted by permission of Faber and Faber Limited

'Stable Song' by Judith Nicholls, from *Magic Mirror* by Judith Nicholls, published by Faber and Faber Limited. © Judith Nicholls 1985. Reprinted by permission of the author

'Christmas at Green Knowe' by Lucy M Boston, from *The Children of Green Knowe* published by Faber and Faber Limited. Reprinted by permission of Faber and Faber Limited

'The Waiting Game' by John Mole, from *Catching the Spider* published by Blackie 1990. © John Mole 1990. Reprinted with the kind permission of the author

'We Three Camels' by Jane Yolen, from *Hark! A Christmas Sampler*, published

Acknowledgements

by G P Putnam & Sons. Copyright © 1991 by Jane Yolen. Reprinted by permission of Curtis Brown Ltd., New York

'Shepherd's Carol' by Norman Nicholson, from *Collected Poems* published by Faber and Faber Limited. © Norman Nicholson. Reprinted by permission of David Higham Associates Limited

'The Thorn' by Helen Dunmore. Reprinted by permission of A P Watt Limited on behalf of Helen Dunmore

'Making the Most of It' by William Kean Seymour, from *Happy Christmas* published by Burkes in 1968. Reprinted with the kind permission of P H K Seymour

'Christmas Ornaments' by Valerie Worth, from *A Christmas Time* published by Michael di Capua (HarperCollins) 1992. © Valerie Worth, the Estate of Valerie Worth Bahkle

'Carol of Patience' by Robert Graves, from *Complete Poems* published by Carcanet Press Limited. Reprinted by permission of Carcanet Press Limited

'Somewhere Around Christmas' by John Smith, found in *Poems for Christmas* published by Hutchinson in 1984

'The Three Drovers' Words by John Wheeler, Music by William James © 1948 Chappell & Co (Australia) Pty Ltd, Australia. Warner Chappell Music Ltd, London W6 8BS. Reproduced by permission of International Music Publications Ltd. All rights reserved

'Ghost Story' by Dylan Thomas, from *The Poems* published by J M Dent. Reprinted by permission of David Higham Associates Limited

'Little Tree' by E E Cummings, from *Complete Poems 1904-1962* by E E Cummings, edited by George J Firmage. © 1991 by the Trustees for the E E Cummings Trust and George James Firmage. Reprinted by permission of W W Norton & Company, London

'The Sheepdog' by U A Fanthorpe, from *Voices Off*, published by Peterloo Poets, Calstock, Cornwall in 1984. © U A Fanthorpe. Reprinted with the kind permission of U A Fanthorpe

'Jubilate Herbis' by Norma Farber. Copyright © Tom Farber. Reprinted by permission of The Stefanidis Agency Inc, Portland, Oregon

'The Holly Bears a Berry' by Alison Uttley, from *Cuckoo Cherry Tree*. Copyright © Alison Uttley Literary Property Trust, 1943. Reprinted by permission of Charles Russell, Solictors on behalf of the Trust

'The Wicked Singers' by Kit Wright, from *Rabitting On*. Copyright © Kit Wright. Reprinted with the kind permission of the author

'Mice in the Hay' by Leslie Norris, from *Norris's Ark* published by The Wells College Press, New York, 2000. © Leslie Norris. Reprinted with the kind permission of the author

'Christmas Eve' by Sandy Brownjohn, from *Both Sides of the Catflap*, published by Hodder Children's Books in 1996. Copyright © Sandy Brownjohn. Reprinted by permission of Hodder and Stoughton Limited

'Merry Christmas' by Aileen Fisher, from *Feathered Ones and Furry* by Aileen Fisher. Copyright © 1971 by Aileen Fisher. Copyright renewed © 1999 Aileen Fisher. Used by permission of Marian Reiner, on behalf of the author

'Christmas Card' by Ted Hughes, from *Season Songs* published by Faber and Faber Limited. Reprinted by Faber and Faber Limited

'Winter Night' by Edna St Vincent Millay, from *Selected Poems* published by Carcanet Press Limited. Reprinted by permission of Carcanet Press Limited

'Questions on Christmas Eve' by Wes Magee, from *The Witch's Brew and other poems* published by Cambridge University Press, 1989. Copyright © Wes Magee 1989. Reprinted with the kind permission of the author

'The Goose is Getting Fat' by Michael Morpurgo. Copyright © Michael Morpurgo. Reprinted with permission of David Higham Associates Limited